South Carolina Native Americans

A Kid's Look at Our State's Chiefs, Tribes, Reservations, Powwows, Lore, and More From The Past and the Present

By Carole Marsh

Native American Heritage™

Graphic Design: Lynette Rowe • Cover Design: Victoria DeJoy

©2004 Carole Marsh/Gallopade International/www.gallopade.com/South Carolina Indians A-Z

Copyright © 2004 Carole Marsh
Permission is hereby granted to the individual purchaser or classroom teacher to reproduce materials in this book for non-commercial individual or classroom use only. Reproduction of these materials for an entire school or school system is strictly prohibited.

Published by
GALLOPADE™
INTERNATIONAL
800-536-2GET
www.gallopade.com

Gallopade is proud to be a member of these educational organizations and associations:

The National School Supply and Equipment Association (NSSEA)
American Booksellers Association (ABA)
Virginia Educational Media Association (VEMA)
Association of Partners for Public Lands (APPL)
Museum Store Association (MSA)
National Association for Gifted Children (NAGC)
Publishers Marketing Association (PMA)
International Reading Association (IRA)
Association of African American Museums (AAAM)

Native American Heritage™ Series

Native American
Big Activity Book

Native American
Biographies

Native American
Coloring Book

Native American
Heritage Book

Native American
Timeline

South Carolina State Stuff™

- My First Pocket Guide: South Carolina
- My First Book About South Carolina
- South Carolina Coloring Book
- The Big South Carolina Reproducible Activity Book
- Jeopardy: Answers & Questions About Our State
- South Carolina "Jography!": A Fun Run Through Our State
- South Carolina Gamebooks
- South Carolina Bingo Games
- South Carolina Illustrated Timelines
- South Carolina Project Books
- South Carolina Bulletin Board Set
- South Carolina PosterMap
- South Carolina Stickers
- Let's Discover South Carolina! CD-ROM

©2004 Carole Marsh/Gallopade International/www.gallopade.com/South Carolina Indians A-Z

Word from the Author

Hello!

I hope you are as interested in North America's wonderful Indian heritage as I am!

Like most kids, I grew up thinking of Indians as the other half of Cowboys. Today, of course, we are getting a much clearer and more accurate picture of what the first peoples on our land were all about. These "facts" are much more fascinating than anything Hollywood can make up. And you probably won't find much of this information in your history textbook!

I am 1/16 Cherokee. This is something I am very proud of and happy about. My grandmother was 1/4 Cherokee. She had tan skin, long gray hair and a very Indian look – especially if I did something bad! Her maiden name was Carrie Corn. Of course, when she got married, she took her husband's name, so it was many years before I learned to appreciate the significance of my native heritage.

Today, I'm trying to make up for lost time by exploring my roots as deeply as I can. One of the most interesting things I've learned is how fascinating all of the Indian tribes are – in the past, the present and future!

As you read about "your" Indians, remember that all native peoples were part of an ever-changing network of time, ideas, power and luck — good and bad. This is certainly a history that is not "dead," but continues to change – often right outside our own back doors! – all the time.

Carole Marsh
She-Who-Writes

PS: Many references show different spellings for the same word. I have tried to select the most common spelling for the time period described. I would not want to be in an Indian spelling bee!

©2004 Carole Marsh/Gallopade International/www.gallopade.com/South Carolina Indians A-Z

A is for . . .

Autumn Green Corn

The annual Cherokee harvest festival.

Awl

An Indian's "needle." Often made from wood, thorns, bone, or metal, it was used to punch holes in skins so they could be sewn together.

Adze

An Indian woodworking tool used to cut, scrape, or gouge; often used to hollow dugout canoes. Blades were made of stone, shell, bone or copper.

Appalachian Mountains

The mountains in western South Carolina are part of this mountain chain, and the Cherokee lived in the foothills. In the 1600s, it was in these mountains that the Cherokee had their first contact with white traders.

Ashtabula

Indian name for "fish river"; today a restored lowcountry plantation near Pendleton in northwest South Carolina.

Altar

A platform made of rocks or animal skulls; some had bowls, feathers, rattles, or skins on them. Indians prayed at these altars for things like good crops or expert hunting skills.

Arrow

A long, slender shaft made of reed, cane, or wood; pointed tip was attached to one end and split feathers to the other. Feathers helped the arrows fly straight.

Ashepoo

An extinct tribe that was a subdivision of the Cusabo tribe. Lived along the lower Ashepoo River in today's Colleton County. The Ashepoo River and the Ashepoo community are named for them.

Aborigine

A member of the earliest known population of a region.

Arrowhead

The pointed tip of an arrow, made of bone, antler, wood, or iron. Some tips had barbs that would embed themselves in flesh. These barbs made it difficult for an enemy to remove the arrowhead from a wound.

©2004 Carole Marsh/Gallopade International/www.gallopade.com/South Carolina Indians A-Z

B is for . . .

Bone Comb

A canuga was a ceremonial comb made of bone used to "scratch" ballplayers. Canuga is also the name of two Cherokee towns in South Carolina.

Band

A subdivision of an Indian tribe. In earlier times, a band was sometimes created when part of a tribe split off from the main group. The band also chose new leadership.

Black Drink

The Catawba Indians made this "Carolina Tea" from the leaves of the *Ilex cassine* plant. The plant contained caffeine.

Baskets

Some were woven and others were coiled. Baskets were made from roots, grasses, barks, and other natural materials.

Blowgun

The Cherokee used this weapon that we usually associate with the Pygmy of Africa. The darts were made of thin splints of wood or reed. The end was wrapped in cotton or thistle down.

Bayberry

A plant used by Indians to make candles. The small gray berries were collected and boiled in water. When the wax floated to the top it was skimmed off.

Bone

Animal bones were used by South Carolina Indians to make buttons, whistles and other items.

Bow

Made from wood, horn or bone. South Carolina Indian children learned how to use bows. The bowstring was made from animal gut, rawhide or twisted vegetable fibers.

Beads

Made of wood, shells, claws, minerals, seeds — you name it! Later, the South Carolina Indians traded with white men for glass beads, used in some of their decorative arts.

©2004 Carole Marsh/Gallopade International/www.gallopade.com/South Carolina Indians A-Z

C is for . . .

Chief

Leader of a tribe. Different titles meant different things. Some members were made chief because they owned deeds to land. Chieftainship was often inherited, usually from the mother!

Contact Period

What historians call the era in the 1500s when Native Americans first met Europeans. This meeting changed the lifestyle of the South Carolina Indians more than anyone could ever have anticipated!

Combahee

This small tribe was a subdivision of the Cusabo. Once lived beside the Combahee River in South Carolina. They died out during the early days of settlement from war and disease.

Catawba

Once the most powerful tribe in the Carolinas. Farmers, friendly to the whites. Often at war with other Indian tribes. War and smallpox reduced their numbers drastically. Fought with the Americans against the British during the Revolutionary War, but their homelands were still taken away. In 1826, most of their reservation was leased to whites. Later, the state of South Carolina bought the rest of their reservation except for 1 square mile! After trying to live in North Carolina, they returned to South Carolina and were finally given 800 acres.

Confederacy

A union of different groups of people. A confederacy in Indian culture was a group of tribes that agreed not to fight with each other. They agreed to live peacefully. Sometimes the tribes shared culture and language.

Cheraw

This Siouan-speaking tribe lived near present-day Cheraw, South Carolina. After large population loss, some merged with the Catawba. Others merged with a group of other Siouan-speaking people to form the Lumbee.

Cusabo

This coastal South Carolina tribe became extinct in the mid 1700s. Had many tribal subdivisions. Along with farming, hunting, and fishing, they kept orchards of peaches and plums!

Cherokee

Lived in the Blue Ridge Mountains of South Carolina in stockaded villages. They farmed communally- owned land and had a government where a tribal council made decisions. The Cherokee have given their name to a county and a falls in South Carolina.

Congaree

Today you can visit the Congarees Historic District near Columbia, named for this lost tribe and site of military operations against the Indians.

Coosa

Muskhogean-speaking Indian tribe of South Carolina; a subdivision of the Cusabo.

©2004 Carole Marsh/Gallopade International/www.gallopade.com/South Carolina Indians A-Z

D is for . . .

Dance

There were Indian dances for every occasion: war, peace, hunting, rain, good harvests, etc. Drums, rattles, and flutes of bone or reed provided the music. Dancers often chanted or sang while performing. Steps were not easy to learn and required consistent practice.

Descendants

The first South Carolina Indians were descendants of primitive hunters who crossed the Bering Strait from Asia to what is now Alaska. At that time, glacial ice still covered most of North America. These people were the true discoverers of the "New World!"

Disease

South Carolina Indians had no immunity to the diseases that white explorers, colonists and settlers brought to their lands. These diseases included smallpox, measles, tuberculosis and others, which ravaged the tribes in great epidemics that killed many, and sometimes all, members of a tribe.

Different Tribes

South Carolina is notable among the southeastern states as being the home of at least 28 different tribes! The tribes altogether spoke five different languages. The coastal plains tribes were small and numerous, while the upcountry are had a few large tribes.

Dyes

Made of lichens, berries, roots, bark, plants, and other natural materials by Indians in South Carolina. Different colors were used depending on what materials were available and what objects were to be dyed.

Dishes

Made from clay, bark, wood, stone, and other materials, depending on what was available and what food they would be used for.

Distinctive Fishing

Some South Carolina Indians fished in a different way. When water levels ran low, they would add special ground-up plants to the water that made fish rise to the surface, belly up!

Dreams

Important in the Indian tradition. It was believed that dreams were the "windows" to the soul. Many thought a person's hidden desires were expressed in dreams.

©2004 Carole Marsh/Gallopade International/www.gallopade.com/South Carolina Indians A-Z

E is for . . .

Eagle

An animal used in many Indian ceremonies. Eagle feathers attached to war bonnets and shields communicated an Indian's rank in his tribe and what kinds of deeds he had done. Feathers also adorned rattles, pipes, baskets, and prayer sticks.

Esaw

Means "river people"; another name for the Catawba tribe.

Estatoee

The name of two former Cherokee settlements. One was located near the meeting of the Tallulah and Chattooga Rivers.

Etiwan

Small Indian tribe, a division of the Cusabo. Their name means "pine tree."

Earrings

Medicine men sometimes pierced male and female ears at special ceremonies. Earrings, which cost parents or relatives a significant amount, symbolized wealth and distinction. The more earrings that an Indian wore, the greater his honor. Some earrings measured 12 inches in length!

Edisto Indians

Tribe that lived on the South Carolina coast near the Edisto River around 1521. Subdivision of the Cusabo. Numbers were depleted by disease and warfare, the tribe disappeared in the early 1700s.

Epidemics

Few Indians possessed immunity to the deadly diseases, like smallpox and measles, which European explorers and settlers brought to the New World. As a result, great population loss took place. Sometimes entire tribes became extinct. Epidemics sparked by Hernando De Soto's expedition are estimated to have killed 75% of the native population in the New World.

Ellijay

The name of a Cherokee town once located on the Keowee River in South Carolina.

©2004 Carole Marsh/Gallopade International/www.gallopade.com/South Carolina Indians A-Z

F is for . . .

Fetish

These small objects were thought to hold the spirit of an animal or a part of nature. A fetish could be an object found in nature, such as bone or wood, or it could be a carved object. The fetish was usually small enough to be carried in a small bag or on a cord. The making and use of a fetish was kept secret by its owner and only shared with the one who inherited it.

Furniture

Indian furniture was very simple. Beds were made of skins laid over a frame of wooden slats; the bed posts were driven into the ground. There was often a storage place over the bed to keep personal items. Stools were made of wood, stone and clay.

Farmers

Many South Carolina Indians, ancient and modern, have farming ways! Even pre-contact Indians tilled and irrigated, raising many important crops. Corn, cotton, beans, squash, melons, sunflowers, gourds, pumpkins and tobacco are all native Indian crops!

Federal Recognition

The United States government's official acknowledgement of a group of Indians as a tribe that is eligible for government benefits, programs and funds.

Fire Drill

A device used by Indians to make fires which consisted of a stick and a piece of wood with a tight hole in it. The stick was twirled rapidly in the hole, creating friction that would ignite shredded grass or wood powder placed nearby to start a fire.

Footwear

South Carolina Indians wore different footwear depending on their tribe and environment. Moccasins were made mostly of animal skin. Sandals were made of rawhide or plant material.

Five Civilized Tribes

The "Five Civilized Tribes" removed to Indian Territory were the Choctaw, Chickasaw, Creek, Seminole, and Cherokee. This name was given to them because of how far they had progressed into adopting the ideas and customs of whites.

©2004 Carole Marsh/Gallopade International/www.gallopade.com/South Carolina Indians A-Z

G is for . . .

Games

Adults played ball and other games of chance or skill. Indian children spun tops, fought pretend battles, did target-shooting, walked on stilts, played hide and seek, or competed to see who could hold their breath the longest!

German Influence

The Cherokee of South Carolina received strong influence from the German settlers who came here to live.

Gueza

An Indian settlement once located in what is today Edgefield County in western South Carolina.

Gens

Group of related members from different tribes.

Gathering

Native Americans gathered natural materials for food, fuel, baskets, clothing, and housing. American Indians tribes also hunted to meet basic needs. Even though some tribes planted crops, most did some kind of gathering.

Gorgets

Beautiful ornaments hung around the neck or from ears; their significance, if any, is unknown.

Gourds

Hollowed-out shell of a gourd plant's dried fruit which often grew into a specific shape. Indians raised many species of gourds. They were used for spoons, bowls, masks, rattles, and even storage.

Greenville

Around 1770, Richard Pearis, who had a Cherokee wife, became the first white trader to settle in the area that would one day become the city of Greenville. A 1777 treaty later gave white settlers like Pearis access to Indian land in the Blue Ridge foothills.

©2004 Carole Marsh/Gallopade International/www.gallopade.com/South Carolina Indians A-Z

H is for . . .

Hair

Indians used hair as a textile. Hair from bison, mountain sheep, elk, moose, deer, dog, rabbit, beaver, or even humans were used to weave cloth, make wigs, or stuff pillows, balls, dolls or drumsticks.

Horn and Hooves

Indians used animal horn to make spoons and dishes. Hooves were made into rattles and bird beaks were used for decoration.

Huspah

A Yamasee band who lived in our area around 1700.

Haiglar

Also called King Haiglar by the English. He was the main chief of the Catawbas. After becoming chief in 1748, he offered to help fight the Cherokee. In 1762, he was killed by the Shawnee.

Hook Indians

This small tribe of Indians once lived on the lower Pee Dee River.

Hoya

Former Indian settlement on the South Carolina coast; name means "raven."

Hickerau

A small Indian village once located on the Santee River.

Houses

Early South Carolina Indians used tree poles covered with bark, grass and palmetto leaves to make houses.

Hominy

Indian food made from corn kernels soaked in water and wood ashes to remove the hull. The kernels were then cooked with meat or fish.

©2004 Carole Marsh/Gallopade International/www.gallopade.com/South Carolina Indians A-Z

I is for . . .

Inisiguanin

Indian town located on the South Carolina coast as early as 1520.

Itseyi

What the whites called several Carolina Cherokee settlements. The name means "green place."

Indian Removal Act of 1830

This federal act gave President Andrew Jackson the power to relocate tribes east of the Mississippi to an "Indian Territory." The forced removal of the southeast Indians later became known as the "Trail of Tears."

Indian Bean

The Catalpa, an ornamental tree, was also called the Indian bean and the candle tree.

Indian Trails

Settlers and traders followed Indian trails into South Carolina. These same trails were the original paths of many of our roads today. Interstate 26 is located on the site of the Cherokee Path which led from the northwest corner of the state to Charleston!

Indian

In 1493, Christopher Columbus called the native people he met in North America "Indians" because he mistakenly believed he had sailed to India! Today, this term includes the aborigines of North and South America.

Indian Ladder

Indians made ladders by trimming branches off a tree. Some were left at consistent intervals to provide steps.

Indian Tribes in South Carolina

At one time or another, these tribes have lived in the state of South Carolina:
Catawba, Cheraw, Cherokee, Congaree, Coree, Cusabo, Eno, Hook, Keyauwee, Pee Dee, Santee, Shakori, Shawnee, Sissipahaw, Tuscarora, Waccamaw, Woccon, Yuchi

©2004 Carole Marsh/Gallopade International/www.gallopade.com/South Carolina Indians A-Z

J is for . . .

Just So You Know . . .

Today you can find many South Carolina Indians that follow some traditional ways. But there are also many who are entrepreneurs, doctors, lawyers, educators and even politicians! If you visit a reservation or cultural event, make sure you know visitor etiquette. Often dances are religious ceremonies and should be observed as such; religious dances should not be applauded. Photography, videotaping and drawing are all important issues - check with the tribe or individual before any is started.

Justice?

For hundreds of years, Native Americans have not received justice from federal and state governments. Native Americans have had nearly all their land taken away. Native Americans still have to fight for their rights in courts across the land..

Jagaya

An early Indian village located in northwest South Carolina around 1565.

Judicial Termination

Modern term to describe current efforts by various U.S. government agencies and officials (especially the judicial system) to legally decrease the sovereignty of independent Indian tribes.

Just In Time!

The Indian Arts and Crafts Act of 1990 makes it against the law to pretend that an item has been made by Native Americans if it is really not. It is illegal to offer or display for sale, or sell any art or craft product in a way that falsely suggests it is Indian produced.

Jerked Meat

Thin strips of buffalo, elk, deer or other animal meat which is dried on racks in the sun; also called "jerky."

©2004 Carole Marsh/Gallopade International/www.gallopade.com/South Carolina Indians A-Z

K is for . . .

Keyauwee

At first this small tribe lived in North Carolina, then Virginia. After that, they moved to the Great Pee Dee River. The tribe is believed to have been absorbed by the Catawba Indians near Rock Hill.

Kulsetsiyi

Once located in Oconee County. This Cherokee settlement was also called Sugartown. The name means "honey locust place." The honey locust was used as a sugar in foods.

Keowee

Several Cherokee Indian towns were given this name in South Carolina. One was in Pickens County; another in Oconee County. These were main settlements of the Lower Cherokee.

Kiawah

This extinct tribe once lived on Kiawah Island near Charleston.

Kusso-Natchez

A small active combined tribe of two distinct groups. They live near the Four Holes area today. The name "Edisto" was adopted for the tribe in 1975, and is not to be confused with the extinct Edisto who were a subdivision of the Cusabo.

Kershaw

Also spelled cashaw, ecushaw and cushaw, this was the Indian word for crooked neck squash.

©2004 Carole Marsh/Gallopade International/www.gallopade.com/South Carolina Indians A-Z

L is for . . .

Linguistic Families

There are 56 related groups of American Indian languages. A few of these speech families include Iroquoian, Algonquian, Siouan, Muskogean, Athapascan, and Wakashan.

Leggings

Both men and women wore cloth or skin covering, which were often decorated with quills, beads, or painted designs, for their legs.

Lost Tribes of Israel

This historic theory has been floating around since 721 BC. The 10 lost tribes of Israel are supposedly groups of people gathered together by Sargon, the King of Assyria. Some say he cast out 10 of the 12 tribes of Israel. Many have tried to prove that the American Indians are these missing tribes!

Land Loss

Native Americans lost their land in many ways. Conflicts with other tribes, colonization, European settlement, treaties, and removal took away Indian lands.

Lodge

The term for a type of Indian house that was usually a permanent dwelling. The population of a tribe was often estimated by its number of lodges.

Lance

Spear used for hunting and war. The hunting lance had a short shaft and a broad, heavy head. The war lance was light and had a long shaft.

Lower Creek

The Indian tribes that lived on the lower Chattahoochee and Alabama Rivers in South Carolina. By 1715 there were around 1,733 Lower Creek Indians. They were also called "Cousin"!

Lariat

These throw ropes made of rawhide, buffalo hair, or horsehair sometimes measured up to 20 feet long!

©2004 Carole Marsh/Gallopade International/www.gallopade.com/South Carolina Indians A-Z

M is for . . .

Maize

Also called Indian Corn. Known as a "cereal" plant because it probably began as some form of grass. The Indians in our state figured out every possible way to use corn as a food. The only thing the white man added was the creation of "corn flakes!"

Mortar and Pestle

A two-part milling tool, with a bowl-shaped stone, plus a club-shaped stone (or wooden bowl and wooden club), used for pulverizing or grinding plants or animal matter.

Moss

Spanish moss was used by the Indians to stuff mattresses!

Maccoa

A small Cusabo division that once lived on the South Carolina coast; they are now extinct.

Moccasins

Indian shoes made of animal skin.

Medicine Man

A person who got the power to heal the sick through a secret means, usually from a dream or visions.

Medicine

Medicine could be good or bad.
Medicines or charms were placed in a bag by young warriors and carried at all times. Some of the roots, leaves and bark that Indians in our state used as medicine are being rediscovered and used by today's doctors!

©2004 Carole Marsh/Gallopade International/www.gallopade.com/South Carolina Indians A-Z

N is for . . .

Nomadic

A way of life in which people frequently moved from one location to another in search of food. "Seminomadic" people had permanent villages, but left them in certain seasons to hunt, fish, or gather wild plant foods.

Newspaper

After the Cherokee Nation got an alphabet in 1821, thousands of Indians learned to read and write in their own language in just a few months! Parts of the Bible were translated into Cherokee. In 1828, the *Cherokee Phoenix* weekly newspaper was printed in both English and Cherokee. It was the first newspaper printed in any North American Indian language.

Nation

There are many Indian nations located within the United States, such as the Cherokee Nation. Indian nations are called nations because their governments and laws are independent of and separate from the U.S. government. The federal government must have "government to government" relations with these Indian nations, just as it would with foreign nations, like England or Spain.

Names

Indian names were often changed during one's lifetime. These names could be derived from events that happened during the person's birth, childhood, adolescence, war service, or retirement from active tribal life. Some names came from dreams, some were inherited, and sometimes names were stolen or taken in revenge. Today some Indians maintain old, traditional Indian names, while others take modern names. Since settlers often did not read or write Indian languages, they recorded Indian names phonetically (as they "sounded"). Thus Indian names were often misspelled.

November

In 1990, President George Bush approved a joint resolution designating November 1990 "National American Indian Heritage Month." Similar proclamations have been issued each year since 1994.

National Museum of the American Indian

The Smithsonian's National Museum of the American Indian on the National Mall in Washington, D.C., symbolizes a deeper understanding between America's first citizens and those who have come to make these shores their home.

Nunna-da-ul-tsun-yi

Cherokee for "the place where they cried"; what the survivors of the forced march to Oklahoma called the path they had traveled. Today we call it the "Trail of Tears."

©2004 Carole Marsh/Gallopade International/www.gallopade.com/South Carolina Indians A-Z

O is for . . .

Oconostota

Former Cherokee chief. He was friendly with the English, but after they mistreated his people, he switched sides to the French. At a battle at Fort Prince George in South Carolina, he and his] warriors fought more than 1,500 soldiers!

Old Estatoee

A former Cherokee settlement located in northwest Oconee County.

Oil

Indians extracted oil from the many layers of fat that came with fresh bear meat. The fat was boiled down in earthen pots to produce the oil, which was stored in gourds and pots. The oil was used for cooking and even beautifying the body! Indians would mix red pigment with the oil, add the fragrances of cinnamon and sassafras, and rub it all over their bodies.

Origins

Some scientists believe that Native Americans actually came across a land bridge between Asia and North America. They say that during an ice age thousands of years ago, the water level was much lower and people could have walked between the two continents.

Otopali

A 1575 Indian village located near present-day Charleston.

Orators

Many Indian leaders were excellent public speakers. Powerful and dramatic speakers were vital to leaders who wanted to influence their tribe. Watch for famous Indian quotations in literature and textbooks!

Office of Indian Education Programs

This is a service organization devoted to providing quality education opportunities for American Indian people. Established in the latter part of the nineteenth century to carry out the federal government's education commitment to Indian tribes, it has become the only national education system for American Indian children and adults.

©2004 Carole Marsh/Gallopade International/www.gallopade.com/South Carolina Indians A-Z

P is for . . .

Powwow

The original form of the word meant "medicine man." Medicine men would often use noise motion and confusion to scare away harmful spirits and cure people. It was also a gathering to talk about political matters. Today, the powwow is an event where Indians gather to sing, perform ceremonial dances, and share cultural pride and traditions.

Play Ball!

South Carolina Indians enjoyed playing a form of ball with rackets that is very similar to the modern-day game of lacrosse! They would put wooden goalposts in the ground. Two teams used sticks to send a stuffed deerskin to each other's goal to score.

Paint

Indians used many natural materials to make paint, like clay mixed with oil or grease. Yellow "paint" was made with the gall bladder of a buffalo! Why did they paint their faces or bodies? Indians used paint to look scary or beautiful, to disguise themselves, or to protect their skin from sunburn or insect bites. Indians often applied red paint because it symbolized strength and success. That is why settlers often referred to the Indians as Red Men.

Pee Dee

A small, active Indian tribe that historically lived in Chesterfield and Marlboro counties. Today the tribe is head-quartered in McColl, South Carolina.

Pemmican

Indian food made of animal meat, which was dried in the sun, pounded together with fat and berries. The mixture was packed into skin bags and used primarily while on the trail.

Papoose

An American Indian infant aged between birth and one year is called a papoose. This word also refers to the way infants were bundled and carried by its mother. A papoose spent most of his or her days snugly wrapped in a kind of cradle made of skins or bark and a wooden frame that hung on the mother's back. This sturdy frame also allowed a mother to lean her papoose against a tree or rock within sight as she worked.

Picture History

Some Indians kept a record of time and important events by painting or drawing pictures or symbols on skin, bark, or stone.

Pottery

Indian pottery was made from built-up spirals of clay that were molded or paddled, or a combination of the two methods. Most pottery served as cooking vessels.

©2004 Carole Marsh/Gallopade International/www.gallopade.com/South Carolina Indians A-Z

Q is for . . .

Quillwork

Indians used the quills of porcupine or birds to make a type of embroidery. Quills were dyed with juice from berries and other materials. When they were ready to be used, the quills were either mashed with teeth or softened with hot water and flattened with rocks. The quills were then laced into moccasins, shirts, pipe covers, and other items. Beads which Indians received by trading with settlers eventually replaced quillwork.

Quality

Native American arts and crafts are known for their excellent craftsmanship and striking designs. This work is often influenced by things found in nature especially plants and animals.

Quiver

Case used to hold arrows; made of woven plant materials or animal skins.

Qualla

The Qualla Arts and Crafts Mutual is a cooperative artists' and craftspeople's organization of 300 Eastern Cherokee artists and craftspeople. Established in 1946, and long recognized as the most outstanding Indian owned and operated arts and crafts cooperative in America!

Quinahaqui

A large Indian village that existed as long ago as the year 1567; located between the Wateree and Catawba Rivers.

©2004 Carole Marsh/Gallopade International/www.gallopade.com/South Carolina Indians A-Z

R is for . . .

Rain Dancing

The rain dance ceremony, performed to encourage rainfall, was common among Indian religions because good weather is vital for a successful harvest. Rainmakers were in tune with nature; there are actual reported cases of Indians producing or preventing rain!

Roots

Indians used plant roots for food, medicine, dye, baskets, cloth, rope, salt, flavoring, and just to chew!

Rattles

Indians of South Carolina made rattles from bird beaks, animal hooves, bones, pods, seashells, turtle shells and other animal parts. The rattles are used in ceremonies.

Red Bones

A tribe of Indians in South Carolina. It is believed they may be related to the Croatan Indians of North Carolina, who may have been descended from Sir Walter Raleigh's mysterious "Lost Colony" of early settlers that vanished with no trace!

Rawhide

Untanned animal hide. The "green" hide was stretched on the ground or over a frame. Flesh and fat were removed. The skin was dried, washed, then buried with wood ashes which made the hair come off. Used by the South Carolina Indian to make drumheads, lash lodge poles, mend broken objects and in many other ways.

Reservations

The U.S. government set aside, or "reserved," land for the Indians. These reservations originally served as a sort of prison during the beginning stages of Indian removal. At that time, reservations provided the government with some control over Indian activity and residency. This land was usually considerably less desirable land than the Indians' native territories. Today's reservations are lands that are tribally held, yet protected by the government.

Removal

The U.S. government policy of the 1830s-1850s that removed Indians from their native lands to new lands, primarily west of the Mississippi River.

©2004 Carole Marsh/Gallopade International/www.gallopade.com/South Carolina Indians A-Z

S is for . . .

Sign Language
A way for Indians to communicate with others from a tribe whose language they did not speak.

Shaman
Medicine man and spiritual leader who was supposed to have special healing power from another world.

Shawnee
Once lived in South Carolina. Their name means "southerners." Were enemies to the Catawbas.

Sweatlodge
Structure used for ritual purification by sweating from exposure to very hot fires or hot steam from pouring water over hot stones. Also called a sweathouse, for some tribes also doubling as clubhouses.

Sequoya
This famous inventor of the Cherokee alphabet believed that writing and printing were very important to the white man, and would be so to the Indian.

Sewee
Small tribe, now extinct, that lived on the Santee River.

Stono
Small extinct tribe; a division of the Cusabo. Lived near Charleston, and was raided by the English to get slaves!

Saltketchers
Yuchi village located in South Carolina around 1715.

Santee
Tribe that lived along the Santee River. In the early 1700s, many Santee were captured and sent as slaves to the West Indies. In the mid 1800s, some Santee joined the Catawba tribe and moved to Oklahoma. Today the South Carolina tribe is actively seeking federal recognition.

Silver Bluff
Former Yuchi village on the Savannah River in Barnwell County.

Sugeree
Small tribe that lived near Rock Hill.

©2004 Carole Marsh/Gallopade International/www.gallopade.com/South Carolina Indians A-Z

T is for . . .

Tobacco

A sacred plant early Indians used to make offering to their gods, cure diseases, bring good luck, seal agreements and bind treaties.

Treaties

Written agreements between the U.S. government and the Indians, most of which involved the Indians giving up their native lands.

"Three Sisters"

What Indians called the important crops of corn, beans and squash.

Totem

The spirit of some natural object (usually an animal) taken by an Indian, tribe or family to guard over them.

Tomahawk

A club, axe or hammer used to chop wood, drive stakes in the ground or as a weapon.

Tugaloo Tribe

Chagee was a Cherokee settlement near the mouth of the Tugaloo River in northwestern South Carolina.

Tracking

To follow a trail by finding a sign such as a broken blade of grass, a moved stone or moccasin track. Indians learned to trail as children, so that they could find food, track enemies and disguise their own signs.

Teeth

South Carolina Indians hung teeth on cords to make necklaces.

Tuscarora

The Tuscarora's ancestral homelands were in the Carolinas. They were friendly with the colonists, taught them much and helped them survive. In return, settlers took the best Tuscarora farmland, cheated them in trading, kidnapped and sold them as slaves in the Caribbean. The Indians began raiding in retaliation, and both Carolinas raised a militia to fight them. This was called the Tuscarora War, and those who survived migrated north to become the Sixth Nation in the Iroquois League in New York.

Tribe

A group of Indians with shared culture, history, original territory, ancestry, social organization, and governmental structure. A tribe may contain several bands of Indians.

Trail of Tears

In the winter of 1838-1839, the U.S. Army rounded up most of the Cherokee and marched them west in horrible weather. At least 1/4 of the Indians (4,000 of them!) died during this trip.

©2004 Carole Marsh/Gallopade International/www.gallopade.com/South Carolina Indians A-Z

U is for . . .

U.S. Bureau of Indian Affairs

Provides public services such as law enforcement, land records, economic development, and education to Indians. Known for mismanagement and ethical problems.

U.S. Army

Many Native Americans have fought bravely for the United States Army. Many have also given their lives for a country that was not always accepting of them.

Unique

Each and every tribe has its own unique customs, language, and traditions.

U.S. Indian Schools

The Bureau of Indian Affairs operates hundreds of federal schools around the nation. Enrollment of Native American children measures in the thousands!

U.S. Indian Reorganization Act

Passed by Congress in 1934, the act authorized Indian tribes to establish and conduct their own governments, and to form businesses.

U.S. President

Once called Great White Father by Indians.

U.S. Colonists

Called Long Knives or Big Knives by early Indians, who also called English explorers "Coat Men."

U.S. Indian Wars

The U.S. War Department has compiled an official list of "Indian Wars" that occurred in the United States. Over 50 wars were fought between the U.S. and the Indians during the period of 1790-1850.

©2004 Carole Marsh/Gallopade International/www.gallopade.com/South Carolina Indians A-Z

V is for . . .

Vessels

Indians carried water in special gourds shaped liked bottles, called water vessels.

Village Councils

These were held in the town (council) house and occurred to discuss and decide important matters. Harmony and agreement was essential to tribal unity. Rather than vote on issues, they were discussed until everyone was satisfied. Anyone who wanted to could speak freely. Everyone did not always agree on the outcome, but everyone avoided conflict by pushing their case.

Vegetable Dyes

Indians could not buy color from the store like we can today. Instead, they created many different colors from the things they found on earth like plants, flowers, shrubs, trees, roots, and berries. They made beautiful and unique reds, oranges, yellows, greens, browns, and violets. These dyes were used for baskets, pottery, weaving, body makeup, and clothing.

Very Hungry

There were Indians who here hunters, gatherers and foragers, that often ate whatever they could find! How hungry would you have to be to eat what they sometimes ate: reptiles, larvae, and insects?

Villages

Many South Carolina Indians lived in villages! Villages were formed around different clans or bands within the tribe, but could also contain different clans living together. Villages were usually permanent settlements, although semi-nomadic tribes have been known to migrate between permanent villages.

Vesperic Indians

Indian tribes located in the United States.

©2004 Carole Marsh/Gallopade International/www.gallopade.com/South Carolina Indians A-Z

W is for . . .

Waxhaw
A South Carolina tribe that once practiced "head-flattening"!

Winyah Bay
Site of early exploration by the Spanish, who had been led there by Indian stories of gold!

Waccamaw
Small South Carolina tribe, still active today, that once lived on the Waccamaw River.

Winyah
Extinct tribe; once lived on the Lower Pee Dee River.

Wateree Indians
The extinct Wateree tribe lived along the Santee and Wateree Rivers in South Carolina. After the 1715 Yamasee War, there were so few of them left that they moved in with the Catawba Indians.

Wampum
Algonquian word for "white." This described beads or strings of beads made of clam or whelk shells. They were used in trade between the Indians and settlers. In 1640, counterfeit wampum was made!

Willow Bark
South Carolina Indians made a type of aspirin from the bark of this tree!

War Club
A weapon made of stone, bone, or wood in the shape of a club.

White Man
Indians generally called them Pale Face, a name the white men themselves suggested!

Westo
South Carolina Indians who once lived on the coast; began to disappear around the early 1700s.

©2004 Carole Marsh/Gallopade International/www.gallopade.com/South Carolina Indians A-Z

XYZ are for . . .

Yuchi

This tribe once lived in the Carolinas. They cultivated fields near streams, made pottery and lived in wigwams made of bark.

Yamasee

Early Indian tribe that revolted when missionaries wanted to take them to the West Indies as slaves. They came to South Carolina to live under the English, but they were treated poorly and fought back. Their special stroke with a paddle in a canoe became known as the Yamasee Stroke.

Yamasee War

Fought between 1715 and 1717, the Indians tried to destroy the new town of Beaufort, since they could see that the settlers would just take more and more of their native homelands for their own. The Indians were defeated by the colonists.

ZZZZZZ...

Shamans and medicine men were not the only people who had access to the spirit world. Indians believed that people could make contact with spirits every night in their dreams! Dreamers could travel back to the time of man's creation or far ahead into their own futures. They also believed that dreams contained warnings or commands from the spirits. Many tribes felt that they had to act out their dreams as soon as they awoke. If an Indian dreamed about bathing, for example, he would run to his neighbors' houses first thing in the morning, and his neighbors would throw kettles full of cold water over him.

Yopon

Also spelled yaupon. A type of coastal holly that a drink was prepared from, also called "black drink" by the English.

Y... Or, "Why?"

1. Why do you think Indian warriors carried charms with them? Some Indian medicines have been scientifically proven to have true healing power and are still used today. Do you think their charms had any real power to help them win battles?
2. Why do you think the American government kept relocating Indians onto reservations and then making the reservations smaller and smaller?
3. Why did Indians use items such as a pipe in ceremonies? What kinds of symbolic objects do we use in ceremonies today?
4. Why and how did Indians use natural materials in creative ways?
5. Many Indian tribes are running successful businesses on their reservations today. There is one industry that many tribes are making a lot of money at. Do you know what this is? Hint:"I'll bet you do!"

©2004 Carole Marsh/Gallopade International/www.gallopade.com/South Carolina Indians A-Z

Which Famous Native American Am I?

Solve the puzzle!

Word Bank

Black Elk	Crazy Horse	Sitting Bull	Sequoia
Sacajawea	Chief Joseph	Geronimo	Pocahontas

Down

1. This Shoshone woman joined Lewis and Clark as their guide and translator and helped make the expedition a success! Hint: She has 4 "a"s in her name!
4. This man gave the Cherokee their first alphabet so that they could write. Until then, they communicated only by speaking and drawing pictures. Hint: A famous ancient tree also has the same name!
5. He was one of the fiercest of Indian warriors! He fought against white settlers in Arizona and New Mexico to keep his people from being pushed off their lands. Hint: Jump!

Across

2. A legend says that this brave Algonquian woman saved the life of Englishman John Smith. Hint: Disney produced a movie about her.
3. He fought at Little Bighorn when he was only 13! He was also a wise "shaman" who saw visions and could advise people. Hint: Part of his name is an animal with antlers!
6. He was a great Sioux warrior who won the battle against General Custer at Little Bighorn in 1876. Hint: His horse was not crazy!
7. A leader of the Lakota (Sioux) tribe who lived on the Standing Rock Reservation in North Dakota after the battle of Little Bighorn. He tried to make conditions better for his people there, so the U.S. government called him a "troublemaker." Hint: He did not sit all the time!
8. A wise and brave chief of the Nez Percé who tried to bring his people to Canada to escape war. He said, "From where the sun now stands, I will fight no more forever." Hint: His father's name was "Old Joseph."

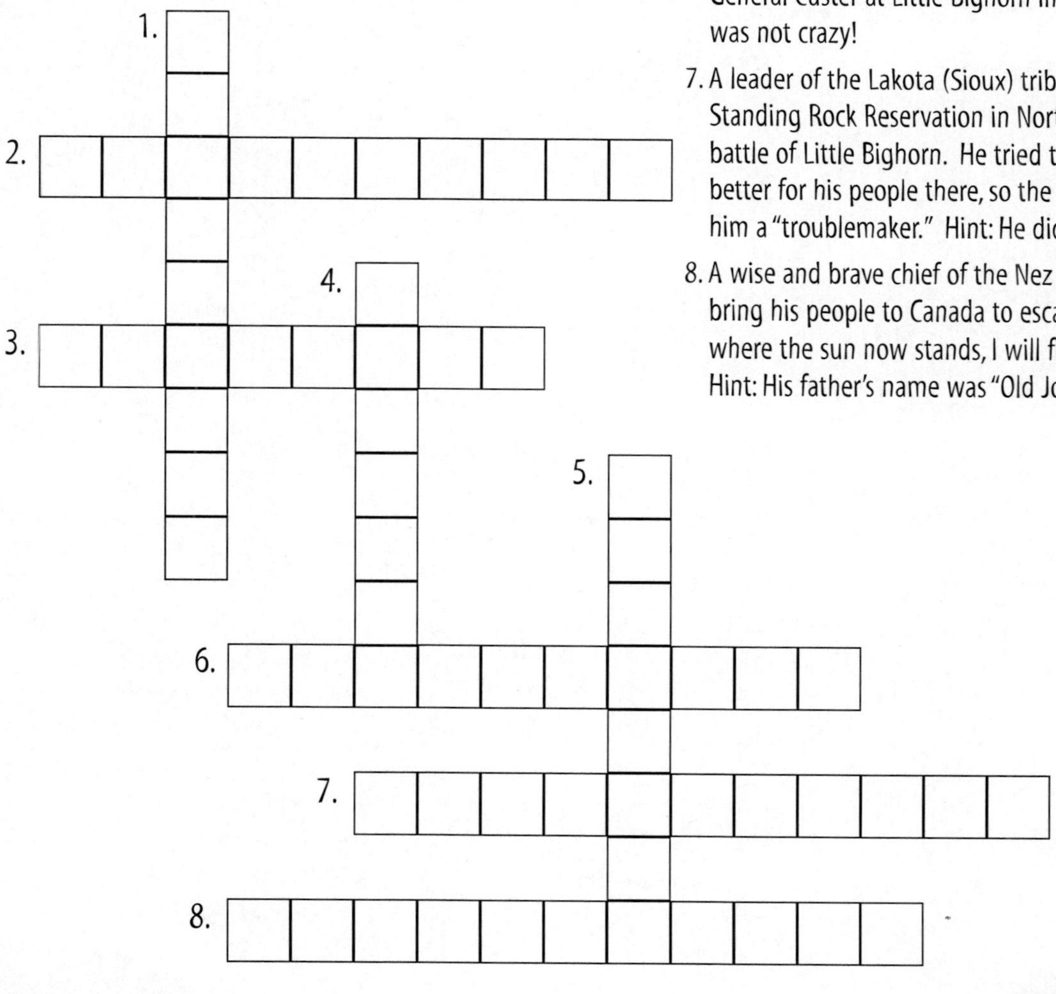

Answer Key: 1. Sacajawea; 2. Pocahontas; 3. Black Elk; 4. Sequoia; 5. Geronimo; 6. Crazy Horse; 7. Sitting Bull; 8. Chief Joseph

©2004 Carole Marsh/Gallopade International/www.gallopade.com/South Carolina Indians A-Z

Different Ways for Different Indians!

North American Indian tribes are divided into different areas. In each of these areas, tribes shared common ways of living with each other. They might make similar arts or crafts, they might eat the same foods, or they might have had the same beliefs. These activities are all part of their "culture." Each area had its own culture, which was different from the tribes in all the other areas.

Below is a map of all the different groups of Indian tribes in North America. Color each area with a different color. You will see a colorful picture of how Native Americans can all be called "Indians" but still have very different cultures!

©2004 Carole Marsh/Gallopade International/www.gallopade.com/South Carolina Indians A-Z

Celebration!

Powwows are big festivals where Native Americans gather to sing, dance, and eat together. It is a time to celebrate and show pride in their culture. Powwows can last from one afternoon to several days. The Indians dress in native costumes and dance ancient dances to the beating of drums.

Artists sell their arts and crafts. You might be able to buy some real Native American food cooked on an open fire. Native Americans go to powwows to be with each other, share ideas, and just have fun! Most powwows are also open to people who are not Indian. It's a great place to learn about Native American culture!

If you went to a powwow this weekend, what do you think you would see? What do you think might NOT be there? Circle the objects you think you would see at a powwow. Put an X through those you probably won't see.

Answer Key: Circled objects are: beads, moccasins, open fire, drums, feathers, baskets, kids, food, drums, horse.

©2004 Carole Marsh/Gallopade International/www.gallopade.com/South Carolina Indians A-Z

Make an Indian Weaving!

Many Native Americans used weaving to create useful things like sashes (belts), bags, mats, and blankets. They used animal hair to make yarn, and dyed the yarn with natural dyes from fruits and other plants. They also used some plant fibers, like cotton, to make weaving thread.

Weave a small Native American mat of your own. Use different colors of yarn to create a beautiful pattern in your weaving. Place a favorite object on the mat or hang it on your wall!

Prepare the "loom"

Cut a piece of cardboard 5 inches wide and 6 inches long. Along the two 5-inch sides (the "short" sides), have an adult cut slits 1/4 inch deep. These slits should be 1/2 inch apart from each other. So, on each short side you will have 9 slits.

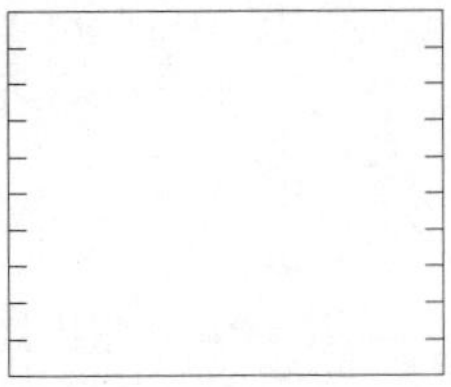

Directions:

1. Take a long piece of yarn and bring it from the back through the first slit (the one next to the edge of the cardboard.) The end of the yarn will hang down behind the cardboard.

2. Bring the yarn right across the front of the cardboard to the slit opposite the one your yarn came through.

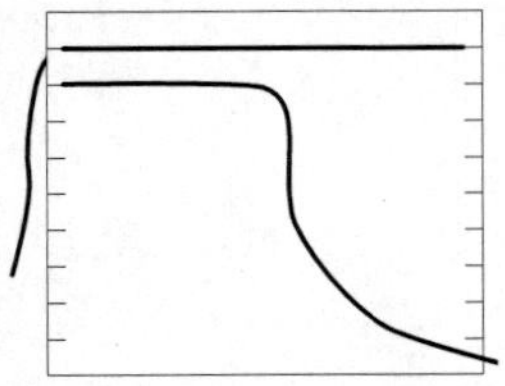

3. Now bring the yarn under the back of the cardboard and then up again through the second slit.

4. Repeat #2 and #3, until you have 9 strands of yarn across the front of your cardboard!

5. Then cut the yarn and tie the two loose ends in the back of the cardboard.

6. Take another piece of yarn and start feeding it through the 9 strands, going over one, under the next over the next, etc. When you get to the end, pull the yarn behind the cardboard and around to the front, and begin again. This time, whatever strand you went over, go under. And whatever strand you went under, go over.

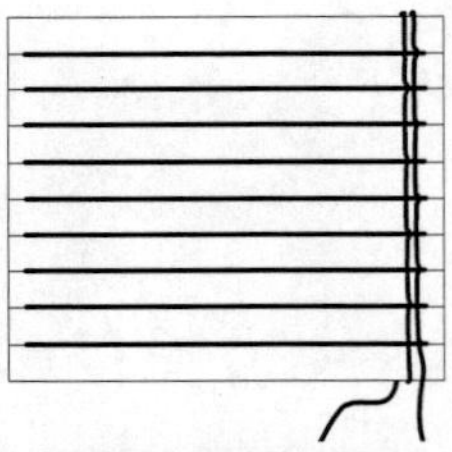

7. Repeat this pattern until the front of your cardboard in covered. Then cut the yarn in the back of the cardboard, and trim it to create a fringe for your mat!

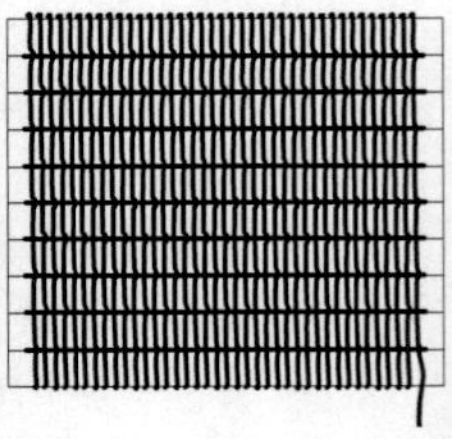

Tips:

- For a wild look, use variegated or different colored yarn!
- For a tighter mat, push the under/over strands up against the previous strands during weaving.
- To keep your mat from unravelling, tie neighboring fringe together up close to the mat.

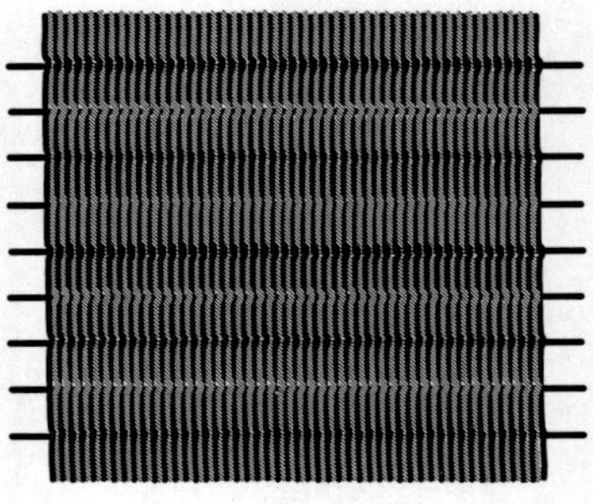

©2004 Carole Marsh/Gallopade International/www.gallopade.com/South Carolina Indians A-Z

Finders Keepers?

Native Americans have many buried treasures. For hundreds of years, special objects would sometimes be buried with Native Americans, or maybe they would just be lost. Archeologists used to dig for interesting artifacts in old Native American gravesites. They would keep the Native American bones or the arrowheads, rattles, masks and other objects that they found. But this made the Native Americans feel like they were being robbed.

In 1990, the U.S. government passed a law that said that no one could look for or take these Native American objects anymore. And whoever had any already had to give them back to the people they belonged to. This is called repatriation

Help the archeologist return the artifact to a Native American.

Fast Fact

An artifact is an object that was made by people a long time ago for some useful purpose.

©2004 Carole Marsh/Gallopade International/www.gallopade.com/South Carolina Indians A-Z

Busy Hands!

Before modern times, Native Americans didn't have stores where they went to buy things. They made everything they needed.

What did Indians make with their own hands? Use the Word Bank and pictures to find out!

Word Bank

blanket	moccasins	arrows	pottery	canoe
mat	food	jewelry	pouch	box

___ ___ ___

___ ___ ___ ___

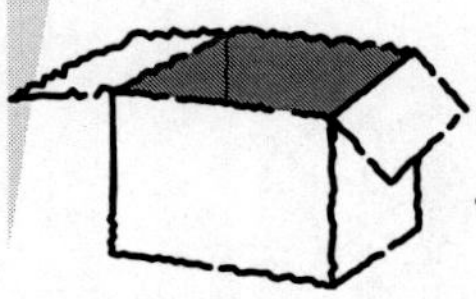
___ ___ ___

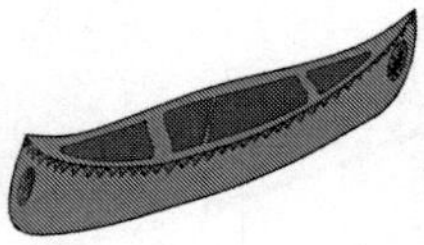
___ ___ ___ ___ ___

___ ___ ___ ___ ___ ___ ___

___ ___ ___ ___ ___

___ ___ ___ ___ ___ ___ ___ ___ ___ ___

___ ___ ___ ___ ___ ___

___ ___ ___ ___ ___ ___ ___

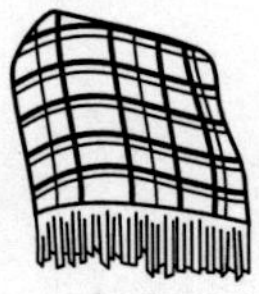
___ ___ ___ ___ ___ ___ ___

©2004 Carole Marsh/Gallopade International/www.gallopade.com/South Carolina Indians A-Z

American Indians Today

Beginning with the first letter of each group of letters, cross out every other letter to discover some new words. You may not have heard of these before, but you can read all about them!

1. Many Indians live on these, but many more do not!

TRYELSDEBRNVJAOTPIPOWNASX

____

2. Many Indians have been poor for a long time because for many years the government took away their lands and their ability to make a living.

TPKOOVWEBRNTXYA

____

3. Many Indians have been studying hard at school and going to college in order to earn more money. Education helps the Indians make their lives better. These Native Americans are working to become:

TSJUMCBCFEYSMSOFPUVL

____

4. This is a big term that means Native Americans have worked hard to get the U.S. government to let them rule themselves. This means that they have their own laws and make their own decisions. They are like a separate country inside the U.S.! Now, try and see if you can get your parents to give you the same thing!

TSGENLBF **JDGEETSEWRAMCIHNUAKTYIKOTNU**

______________ ______________________________

Fast Fact

What do Indians work as today?

- doctors
- nurses
- factory workers
- artists
- lawyers
- actors

The same kinds of jobs any American might work at!

©2004 Carole Marsh/Gallopade International/www.gallopade.com/South Carolina Indians A-Z

Native Americans Move to the City!

Solve the code to discover the mystery words!

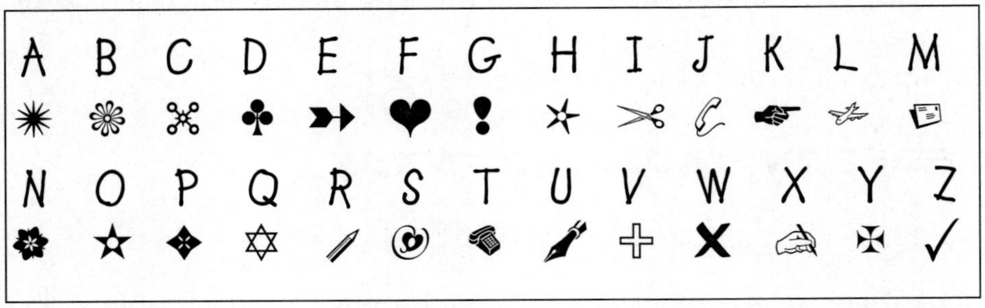

1. During the 1950s and 1960s, the American government paid Indians to leave their homes on reservations and move to cities to get jobs. If cities are sometimes called urban areas, then these brave Indians were called:

___ ___ ___ ___ ___   ___ ___ ___ ___ ___ ___ ___

2. Many Indians chose to stay on their reservations and not move to the city. They thought that if they moved to the city, they would lose the way of life that their parents and ancestors had taught. These Indians called themselves:

___ ___ ___ ___ ___ ___ ___ ___ ___ ___ ___   ___ ___ ___ ___ ___ ___ ___

3. Native Americans who moved to cities lived close to each other. They tried to keep their way of life as much as possible. They did not want to forget their religion, native art, or music. They did not want to lose their:

___ ___ ___ ___ ___ ___ ___

4. Are you afraid of heights? Many people are. The Mohawk Indians are not! Many of them work hundreds of feet above the city to build steel frames for skyscrapers. People who do this work above the city are:

___ ___ ___ ___ ___   ___ ___ ___ ___ ___ ___ ___

5. Today urban Indians and reservation Indians come together to celebrate their culture. They share ideas and stories. They dance and beat drums. They make and sell Indian jewelry. During these celebrations, Indians remember how much they have to be proud of! These big parties are called

___ ___ ___ ___ ___ ___ ___

©2004 Carole Marsh/Gallopade International/www.gallopade.com/South Carolina Indians A-Z